THE OBSESSION

SHYAM SATHISH

Made with ❤ on the Notion Press Platform
www.notionpress.com

Contents

Acknowledgements

I would like to express my deepest gratitude to my editor, who worked tirelessly to shape this story into the best version of itself. I would also like to thank my friends and family for their unwavering support and encouragement throughout the writing process.

Foreword

In "The Obsession," readers are taken on a thrilling and suspenseful journey through the dark and dangerous world of stalking. With expertly crafted characters and a plot that keeps readers guessing until the very end, this novel is sure to keep readers on the edge of their seats. But beyond the page-turning excitement, "The Obsession" also sheds light on the very real and terrifying issue of stalking and the impact it can have on a person's life.

Preface

We all have our secrets. Some we keep hidden away, locked up deep inside us, while others are shared only with those closest to us. But what happens when someone else knows our secrets, and uses them against us?

This is the story of Claire, a successful businesswoman who seems to have it all - a loving husband, a beautiful home, and a thriving career. But when she begins to receive anonymous letters and gifts from a stalker, she realizes that her perfect life may not be what it seems.

As Claire's obsession with finding her stalker grows, she is forced to confront her deepest fears and darkest secrets. The journey she takes is not an easy one, and it is full of twists and turns that will keep you guessing until the very end.

This book is a psychological thriller, a story of one woman's fight to protect the life she has built for herself, and a warning about the dangers of obsession. I hope that you will join me on this journey with Claire, and that you will find the story as gripping and suspenseful as I have.

Remember, sometimes the greatest danger comes from within, and the only way to overcome it is to face it head-on.

Prologue

Claire had always been cautious about her personal safety. As a successful businesswoman, she knew that her position made her a potential target for those who would do her harm. But nothing could have prepared her for the terror that awaited her when the letters began to arrive.

CHAPTER ONE

The Perfect Life

Claire wakes up to the sound of birds chirping outside her bedroom window. She stretches and looks at her husband, who is still sleeping soundly beside her. She smiles and thinks about how lucky she is to have such a wonderful life. She gets out of bed and walks to the window, admiring the beautiful view of the ocean from her bedroom.

As she gets ready for work, she thinks about all the things she needs to do that day. She has an important meeting with a new client and needs to prepare a presentation. She also needs to make dinner reservations for her and her husband at a fancy restaurant for their anniversary.

Claire arrives at work and is greeted by her assistant, who hands her a cup of coffee and a stack of messages. She starts going through her emails and notices one from an unknown sender. It's a short message that simply says, "I'm watching you."

At first, Claire brushes it off as a prank or a mistake. But as the day goes on, she receives more emails and letters from the same sender. The messages become more personal and more threatening, and Claire starts to feel like someone is watching her every move.

As she leaves the office that day, she notices a man standing across the street, staring at her. She tries to ignore him and walks quickly to her car. As she drives home, she can't shake the feeling that she is being followed.

When she gets home, she tells her husband about the emails and letters. He tries to reassure her and suggests that they go to the police, but Claire brushes it off, not wanting to make a big deal out of it.

The next day, Claire receives another letter, this time with a gift - a single red rose. She starts to feel even more uneasy and decides to hire a private investigator to help her find out who is behind the messages and gifts.

As she lays in bed that night, Claire can't shake the feeling that her perfect life is starting to unravel. She worries about what the stalker might do next and wonders if she will ever be able to feel safe again.

CHAPTER TWO

First Letter

The letter arrived on a Tuesday. Claire recognized the handwriting on the envelope right away, but couldn't place it. She tore open the envelope and unfolded the thick, creamy paper inside.

"Dear Claire," the letter began. "I have been watching you for some time now, and I must say, I'm quite taken with you. You have everything I could ever want, and I want it all for myself."

Claire felt a chill run down her spine as she read the words. She scanned the rest of the letter, which went on to describe in detail all of Claire's daily activities, from her morning jog to the color of the dress she wore to a recent party. The letter ended with a threat.

"Be careful, Claire," it read. "I'm always watching."

Claire's hands shook as she put down the letter. She couldn't believe that someone had been watching her, following her, and knew so much about her life. She tried to shake it off and continue with her day, but she couldn't shake the feeling of being watched.

Over the next few days, more letters arrived. They were all from the same anonymous sender, but they grew increasingly threatening. The writer claimed to know everything about Claire's life, and warned her not to tell anyone about the letters or bad things would happen.

Claire tried to tell her husband, but he didn't take her seriously. He thought she was overreacting and suggested she see a therapist. Claire felt alone and afraid, with nowhere to turn.

As the days went on, the letters grew more and more disturbing. They contained graphic descriptions of what the writer wanted to do to Claire, and promised that it was only a matter of time before they would be together.

Claire's world was turned upside down. She could barely sleep, she was always looking over her shoulder, and she had lost all sense of safety and security. She knew she had to do something, but she didn't know what.

In the coming days, Claire's obsession with finding out who was behind the letters would drive her to dangerous lengths, putting herself and those around her in harm's way. As the situation escalated, Claire would have to confront the terrifying truth behind the letters and the danger that threatened to consume her life.

The next day she recieved a small box.

CHAPTER THREE

A Gift and a Threat

Claire sat at her desk, staring at the small box that sat in front of her. It was wrapped in shiny silver paper and tied with a red ribbon, and a small card sat on top. She had found it sitting on her doorstep when she had arrived home from work the day before. At first, she had assumed it was a gift from her husband, but when she had opened the card, her blood had turned to ice.

The card was plain white, with black lettering that simply read, "I know what you've been doing."

Claire had spent a sleepless night, her mind racing with fear and anxiety. She had no idea who could have sent the gift or what they wanted from her. Was it a co-worker who was jealous of her success? An ex-boyfriend with a grudge? Or was it someone even closer to her, someone she had trusted and confided in?

The box sat there, taunting her. She knew she should call the police, but she didn't want to involve them until she knew more. She wanted to find out who was behind this on her own.

With shaking hands, she picked up the box and carefully unwrapped it. Inside was a single, blood-red rose. It was beautiful and fragrant, but it filled Claire with a sense of dread.

She sat there for a long time, staring at the rose and trying to make sense of it. Finally, she decided to take action. She couldn't just sit there and wait for the stalker to strike again.

She made an appointment to see a private investigator the next day. She had found his name online and he had good reviews. She wasn't sure if he could help her, but she was desperate for answers.

The rest of the day passed in a blur. Claire couldn't focus on her work, and every sound made her jump. She felt like she was being watched at every moment.

That night, she sat down with her husband and told him everything. He was shocked and angry, but he promised to support her and help her in any way he could.

As they sat there talking, the phone rang. Claire's heart jumped into her throat as her husband answered it.

"It's for you," he said, holding out the phone.

Claire took the phone, her hand shaking. She put it to her ear and said, "Hello?"

The voice on the other end was distorted and unrecognizable, but the words were clear.

"I hope you enjoyed my gift," the voice said. "There will be more to come."

CHAPTER FOUR

Increasing Paranoia

As the anonymous letters and gifts continue to arrive, Claire's anxiety and paranoia increase. She starts to question everyone around her and second-guess every interaction, wondering if they could be her stalker. She finds herself looking over her shoulder constantly and jumps at every unexpected noise or movement.

At work, she has trouble focusing on her tasks and finds herself making mistakes. Her colleagues notice her distracted behavior and express their concern, but Claire is too embarrassed to admit what is happening. Instead, she tells them that she is dealing with some personal issues and that it is affecting her concentration.

At home, Claire's relationship with her husband starts to suffer. She becomes more distant and less affectionate, leading him to believe that she is having an affair. He confronts her about it, but she brushes it off and blames it on stress from work.

As the letters become more threatening, Claire realizes that she can no longer keep this to herself. She confides in her best friend, who encourages her to go to the police. But Claire is hesitant. She fears that going to the police will only make things worse and that the stalker will retaliate.

Instead, she takes matters into her own hands and starts to research self-defense techniques. She takes up kickboxing and buys pepper spray. She starts to feel more empowered, but she knows that these measures are only temporary solutions.

Claire becomes increasingly desperate for answers. She starts to obsessively research the stalker's handwriting, trying to match it to someone she knows. She pours over every detail of the letters and gifts, trying to find a clue that will lead her to the stalker's identity.

But as she gets closer to the truth, she realizes that the stalker is much closer to her than she ever could have imagined. The revelation sends her into a panic, and she realizes that her life is in danger. She must find a way to escape her stalker's grasp before it's too late.

CHAPTER FIVE

Trust Issues

As the anonymous letters and disturbing gifts continue to pile up, Claire becomes increasingly paranoid and suspicious of everyone around her. She can't help but wonder if her stalker is someone she knows and trusts, perhaps even her own husband.

At work, Claire finds it difficult to concentrate and her colleagues start to notice her erratic behavior. She begins to second-guess every decision she makes and feels like everyone is watching her every move. The once-confident businesswoman is now a shadow of her former self, constantly looking over her shoulder and jumping at every sound.

At home, her relationship with her husband starts to strain under the weight of her paranoia. She can't help but question his every move and motive, wondering if he is the one behind the threats. They argue more often, and the once-loving relationship turns tense and uncomfortable.

Claire decides to confide in her best friend, but even she starts to suspect that Claire might be losing her mind. As the threats escalate and the tension mounts, Claire begins to wonder if she can trust anyone at all.

One day, Claire receives a call from an unknown number. She answers tentatively, and to her surprise, it's the private investigator she had hired to help her with the case. He has some new information, but he can't discuss it over the phone. He asks Claire to meet him in person, but she is hesitant. Can she trust him? Or is he in on it too?

In the end, Claire decides to meet with the investigator, hoping that he can help her get to the bottom of the threats. But as she heads to the meeting, she can't shake the feeling that she might be walking into a trap. Will she be able to trust anyone in her search for the truth? Or will her obsession with the stalker lead her down a dangerous path?

CHAPTER SIX

Turning Point

Claire had been living with the fear of her stalker for weeks now. She had changed her daily routine, installed extra security measures, and tried to stay alert at all times, but the anxiety was starting to take its toll on her. She was tired of living in constant fear and wanted to take control of the situation.

One night, as she was working late in her office, Claire heard a noise coming from the hallway. She froze, listening intently for any sign of movement. When she heard the sound again, she knew that she couldn't ignore it any longer.

Taking a deep breath, Claire got up from her chair and slowly made her way to the door. As she opened it, she saw a shadow moving in the darkness. Her heart pounding in her chest, she flipped on the light switch and came face to face with her stalker.

For a moment, time stood still as the two of them stared at each other. Claire felt like she was in a dream, unable to move or speak. The stalker, a man she had never seen before, was dressed in black and had a mask over his face.

But then, in a sudden burst of courage, Claire reached for the pepper spray she kept in her desk drawer and sprayed it at the man. He stumbled back, blinded by the spray, giving Claire just enough time to run for the door and call for help.

The police arrived within minutes, but the stalker had already fled. Claire was left shaken but relieved that she had finally taken action. She knew that she couldn't continue to live in fear, and that it was time to find out who was behind the threats and put an end to it once and for all.

Over the next few days, Claire worked with her private investigator to piece together any information that could lead to the stalker's identity. She looked through old emails and texts, interviewed coworkers, and even searched her own home for clues.

But just when Claire thought she had a lead, she received another letter from the stalker. It was a chilling reminder that he was still out there, watching her every move, and that the game was far from over.

CHAPTER SEVEN

The Private Investigator

Claire had finally decided that she couldn't handle the situation on her own. She needed professional help. She had gone to the police but they told her there was nothing they could do as there was no concrete evidence. She had a feeling that whoever was stalking her was watching her closely and that they would never slip up enough to be caught. She was running out of options.

One evening, after much consideration, she made the decision to hire a private investigator. She knew that it would be expensive, but she was willing to pay any price to bring her tormentor to justice.

She searched online for private investigators in her area and finally found a reputable firm with high ratings. She called them the next day, and after a brief discussion, she was assigned a private investigator named James.

James was a former police officer with years of experience in handling cases just like hers. Claire met him at a café and discussed everything she knew about her stalker. She gave him all the letters and gifts that she had received, hoping that it would provide some lead. James told her that he would get to work immediately, and they parted ways.

For the next few days, Claire received frequent updates from James. He had installed cameras around her house to capture any suspicious activities, and was keeping a watch on her every move. She felt a sense of relief knowing that someone was on her side, but at the same time, she was still scared.

One evening, she received a call from James, asking her to meet him at his office the next day. Claire arrived at James' office, and he showed her the footage he had captured on his cameras. They sat together and watched hours of footage, but it didn't provide any conclusive evidence.

Claire started to feel hopeless. She was starting to wonder if there was anything anyone could do to help her. James must have noticed the despair on her face because he quickly reassured her that they would find a way. He said that he had one last idea - a risky one, but it might just work.

He proposed that they try to lure the stalker into revealing their identity by staging a fake attack on Claire. James explained that he would make it seem like the stalker had succeeded in harming Claire, and they could use that to their advantage.

Claire was hesitant at first, but she knew that it was her best chance at catching the stalker. She agreed to go along with the plan, and they spent the next few days meticulously planning the details.

The plan was set in motion a few nights later. Claire was nervous, but she trusted James. She hoped that they would be able to finally catch her stalker and put an end to her nightmare.

CHAPTER EIGHT

Closer to the Truth

Claire's life had been turned upside down by the anonymous letters and gifts from her stalker. Her once perfect life was now a living nightmare, and she had no idea who was behind it all. She had hired a private investigator, David, to help her, but so far they had no concrete leads.

David had been working around the clock to gather information and evidence on the stalker. He had interviewed Claire's colleagues, friends, and family, trying to identify anyone who might have a motive to harm her. He had also been monitoring her emails and social media accounts, hoping to catch a clue.

One evening, David called Claire with an urgent message. He had found something significant and needed to see her right away. Claire met David at a small café, where he showed her a surveillance photo taken outside her home the night before. The photo showed a person lurking in the shadows, partially hidden by a tree.

Claire gasped in shock. She had never seen the person in the photo before, but something about their posture and the way they were dressed looked familiar. David pointed out that the person was wearing a hooded jacket and gloves, which would make it difficult to identify them.

David told Claire that he had an idea for how they could catch the stalker. He suggested that they stage a fake attack on Claire, with David playing the role of the attacker. If the stalker was watching, he or she might be lured into revealing themselves.

At first, Claire was hesitant. The idea of putting herself in harm's way was terrifying. But she knew that they needed to do something to catch the stalker and put an end to the harassment. She agreed to the plan.

David and Claire worked out the details of the plan, and they set a date for the fake attack. They decided to stage it in a public place, so that there would be witnesses and plenty of security cameras to capture the action.

The day of the attack arrived, and Claire was a bundle of nerves. She wore a hidden microphone so that David could hear everything that was happening, and she had a panic button in case things went wrong.

As Claire walked down a crowded street, David suddenly appeared from behind a corner, wearing a hooded jacket and gloves. He lunged at Claire, who screamed and fought back with all her might.

The attack was over in a matter of seconds, and David quickly revealed his true identity. The bystanders were shocked, and Claire was left shaken and traumatized.

David looked around, hoping to spot the stalker, but there was no sign of him or her. They had hoped to catch the stalker in the act, but it seemed that the plan had failed.

Claire and David retreated to a nearby café, where they sat in silence, both feeling defeated. Suddenly, David's phone rang. He answered it, and his face lit up with excitement.

"I've got something!" he exclaimed.

Claire's heart leaped with hope. They had finally caught a break. David explained that he had been monitoring Claire's emails and had found an anonymous message sent to her a few days earlier. The message contained a clue that could lead them to the stalker.

With renewed energy, Claire and David set out to follow the clue and track down the stalker. As they raced against time, they knew that they were getting closer to the truth. But they also knew that the stalker was watching and that they had to be careful. They were playing a dangerous game, and the stakes were higher than ever.

CHAPTER NINE

Betrayal

As the private investigator, Jack, delves deeper into the investigation, Claire becomes increasingly nervous. She trusts Jack, but she also knows that the stalker could be anyone - even someone close to her.

One day, Jack comes to her with some unsettling news. He tells her that he's found evidence that points to her husband, Mark, as the prime suspect. Claire is shocked and refuses to believe it, but the evidence is convincing: Mark had motive, opportunity, and had lied to Jack about his whereabouts on the day of one of the incidents.

Claire confronts Mark about the evidence, but he vehemently denies any involvement. He tells her that he loves her and would never do anything to harm her. But Claire is torn - she loves Mark and wants to believe him, but she also can't ignore the evidence.

As the investigation continues, Claire becomes increasingly isolated. She's scared to trust anyone, even her own husband. She starts to doubt her own sanity and wonders if she's overreacting. She also starts to question her own role in the situation - did she do something to provoke the stalker? Is she somehow to blame?

One day, Claire receives a phone call from an unknown number. She answers it, and it's the stalker. He taunts her, telling her that he's been watching her and that he knows everything about her. Claire is terrified and can barely speak, but she manages to ask the stalker why he's doing this. The stalker's response chills her to the bone: "Because you deserve it."

Claire hangs up the phone and collapses in tears. She's never felt so alone and helpless. She starts to think that maybe Jack was right about Mark, but she still can't bring herself to believe it. She feels trapped and suffocated, unable to escape the terror that's consuming her life.

At the end of the chapter, Claire is faced with a choice: does she trust her husband and risk being hurt, or does she turn him in to the police and risk losing everything she's ever known? The decision weighs heavily on her, and she realizes that no matter what she chooses, her life will never be the same.

CHAPTER TEN

The Final Confrontation

As Claire gets closer to the truth about her stalker, she realizes that the danger is much closer than she ever could have imagined. She had suspected everyone from her co-workers to her husband, but it turns out that the person who has been terrorizing her is someone she never would have suspected.

It all starts when Claire's private investigator discovers a clue that leads him to the stalker's location. Claire decides to take matters into her own hands and confront the stalker once and for all. She sets up a meeting at a remote location where she can meet the stalker face-to-face.

As she drives to the meeting, Claire's nerves are on edge. She knows that this could be the most dangerous thing she has ever done, but she is determined to end the nightmare that has taken over her life.

When she arrives at the meeting spot, she sees a figure standing in the distance. As she gets closer, she realizes that it is her stalker, and he is holding a gun.

Claire tries to reason with him, but he is clearly unhinged and delusional. He tells her that he has been in love with her for years and that he was willing to do whatever it took to make her his. He admits to sending the letters and the gifts and says that he did it all out of love.

As Claire backs away, the stalker raises his gun and takes aim. Claire knows that she has only seconds to act. She uses her quick thinking and resourcefulness to disarm the stalker and knock him to the ground.

With the stalker subdued, Claire is finally able to breathe a sigh of relief. She turns him over to the police, who arrest him and charge him with multiple crimes, including stalking and attempted murder.

As she leaves the police station, Claire feels a sense of freedom and relief that she hasn't felt in months. She knows that the road to recovery will be long, but she is determined to move on with her life and put this nightmare behind her.

CHAPTER ELEVEN

Fight for Survival

As the sun sets on the day of the final showdown with her stalker, Claire's heart is racing. She's been on edge for weeks, waiting for this moment, and now it's finally here.

She's sitting in her car outside the abandoned warehouse that the private investigator found as the stalker's hideout. She has a gun in her purse, but she's not sure if she'll be able to use it. She's not a violent person, but she knows that this is a fight for her life.

She gets out of the car and walks toward the warehouse, trying to keep her nerves in check. She sees the door is slightly ajar and hesitates for a moment before pushing it open. The smell of must and decay hits her as she steps inside.

The warehouse is dark, but she can see a faint light coming from a room at the back. She walks quietly toward it, her heart pounding in her chest. As she gets closer, she can hear someone breathing heavily. She raises her gun and steps into the room.

There, she sees the stalker, dressed in black, standing in front of a table with a knife in his hand. He's taken off his mask, revealing his face for the first time. Claire is shocked to see that it's someone she knows, someone she trusted.

"What are you doing here?" the stalker asks, a smirk on his face.

"I'm here to end this," Claire replies, her voice shaking.

The stalker laughs. "You don't have it in you. You're weak. You always have been."

Claire grits her teeth and takes a deep breath. She raises her gun and points it at the stalker. "You don't know me," she says. "You don't know what I'm capable of."

The stalker lunges at her with the knife, and Claire fires her gun. The shot echoes through the warehouse as the stalker falls to the ground. Claire stands there, gun still pointed at the stalker, her heart racing.

CHAPTER TWELVE

Unmasking the Stalker

Claire's heart was pounding as she followed the private investigator's instructions to meet her stalker in a deserted alleyway. She knew that this could be the moment that would put an end to the terror that had been haunting her for months. But she also knew that this was the most dangerous thing she had ever done in her life.

The PI had equipped her with a hidden microphone and a tracking device. She was to pretend that she was alone, without any backup. Her husband had wanted to come with her, but the PI had advised against it, fearing that the stalker might have spies around.

Claire's hands were shaking as she walked towards the designated spot. She was wearing a wire, and every step she took felt like a thousand-pound weight on her chest. She felt like she was walking into a trap, but she had to do this. She had to face her stalker, and she had to find out who he was.

As she got closer to the alleyway, she saw a figure standing in the shadows. She couldn't make out his face, but she could feel his presence. She could feel his eyes on her, watching her every move. She hesitated for a moment, but then she took a deep breath and walked towards him.

"Who are you?" she demanded, her voice trembling.

The stalker stepped out of the shadows, and Claire's heart stopped. It was someone she knew. Someone she trusted. Someone she had never suspected.

"You!" she gasped, her mind racing. "How could you do this to me? How could you be my stalker?"

The stalker smirked. "It was easy. You were so unsuspecting. So trusting. It was fun to watch you squirm."

Claire's mind was reeling. How could someone she had trusted be capable of something so heinous? How could she have been so blind?

She felt a surge of anger, and before she knew it, she had lunged at the stalker, trying to get the microphone closer to his face. But he was quick, and he dodged her, sending her tumbling to the ground.

As she tried to regain her composure, the stalker leaned in close, his breath hot on her face.

"You think you can stop me?" he sneered. "You think you can unmask me? You're nothing. You're nobody. And nobody can stop me."

Claire looked up at him, determination in her eyes. "I can and I will," she said. "You may have fooled me once, but you won't fool me again. I will bring you down, and I will make sure that you pay for what you've done."

With that, she pulled herself up to her feet and ran, with all her might. She knew that she had to get away, and fast. She could hear the stalker's footsteps behind her, but she refused to look back.

When she finally reached the safety of the PI's car, she collapsed into the seat, gasping for breath. She looked over at the PI, who was watching her with concern.

"Did you get everything?" he asked, his eyes fixed on her.

Claire nodded, still trying to catch her breath. "I got everything," she said, her voice shaking. "And I know who he is."

CHAPTER THIRTEEN

Aftershock

Claire sat in her hospital room, staring blankly at the wall. Her face was bruised, her arm was in a cast, and she had bandages wrapped around her head. The doctors had told her that she was lucky to be alive, but Claire didn't feel lucky. She felt broken.

She had been through so much in the past few weeks. The letters, the gifts, the paranoia, the betrayal, the fight for survival - it had all taken a toll on her. And now, to add insult to injury, she was stuck in a hospital bed, unable to move or do anything.

But as Claire sat there, she realized that the worst was not over yet. She still had to face the aftermath of what had happened. She still had to deal with the fact that someone had been stalking her, that someone had been watching her every move, that someone had tried to kill her.

And then there was the guilt. Guilt for not realizing sooner that her husband was involved. Guilt for not trusting her instincts. Guilt for putting her own life in danger.

Claire's thoughts were interrupted by a knock on the door. It was the private investigator she had hired, John. He had been with her every step of the way, helping her uncover the truth about her stalker.

"Hey," John said, walking into the room. "How are you feeling?"

"I don't know," Claire replied. "I feel like everything is a blur. Like I'm in a dream."

"I know it's tough," John said, sitting down next to her. "But you made it. You survived."

Claire nodded, tears welling up in her eyes. "I just can't believe it all happened. I can't believe that someone was so obsessed with me that they would go to such lengths to hurt me."

John took her hand. "I know. It's hard to wrap your head around it. But you're safe now. And we're going to make sure that the person responsible is brought to justice."

"But how do I move on from this?" Claire asked, her voice trembling. "How do I go back to my life, knowing that someone out there wants to hurt me?"

John leaned in closer. "You don't have to do it alone," he said. "You have people who care about you. You have me. And we're going to help you every step of the way."

As John spoke, Claire felt a glimmer of hope. Maybe she could move on from this. Maybe she could put it all behind her and start anew.

CHAPTER FOURTEEN

Moving On

Claire sat in the garden, the sun beating down on her face. It had been six months since her ordeal with the stalker, and she was finally starting to feel like herself again. She had gone through months of therapy to deal with the trauma, but it had been worth it. She had a newfound appreciation for life and was determined to live it to the fullest.

She had resigned from her high-stress job and decided to start her own business. It was a risk, but she knew that she needed to take control of her life and do something that made her happy.

As she sat there, sipping on her coffee, she couldn't help but think about the past. The memories still haunted her, but she was learning to cope with them. She had even started dating again, something she never thought she would do.

Suddenly, her phone rang, interrupting her thoughts. She answered it, and a smile spread across her face as she heard the voice on the other end.

"Hey, Claire, it's Mark. I was wondering if you wanted to grab lunch today?"

Mark was the private investigator she had hired to help her with the stalker. They had become good friends during the ordeal, and he had been a huge support to her.

"Sure, Mark, I'd love to," she replied, standing up and brushing off her dress.

As they sat in the cafe, catching up on each other's lives, Claire couldn't help but feel grateful for everything that had happened. It had been a terrifying experience, but it had taught her so much about herself and the people around her.

"I'm so proud of you, Claire," Mark said, smiling at her. "You've come so far since I first met you."

"Thanks, Mark," she replied, blushing. "I couldn't have done it without you."

They finished their lunch, and as they said goodbye, Claire knew that she was going to be okay. She had survived the worst, and she was stronger because of it. She was moving on, and she was excited for what the future held.

CHAPTER FIFTEEN

The New Problem

Claire had thought that the nightmare was over. She had unmasked her stalker, fought for her life, and survived. But as she tried to move on, a new problem emerged.

One day, while she was at work, she received an email from an unknown sender. The subject line read "I'm still watching you", and the message was just a single sentence: "You may have won the battle, but the war is far from over."

Claire's heart started racing as she read the email. She couldn't believe it. How was this possible? She had taken every precaution to ensure her safety, but somehow her stalker had found a way to contact her again.

For the next few days, Claire was on high alert. She was constantly checking over her shoulder, watching for any signs of danger. She couldn't focus on her work or her personal life. All she could think about was the threat that was looming over her.

Then, things started to get worse. She began receiving more emails, each one more ominous than the last. The stalker had somehow found out where she worked, where she lived, and even who her friends were. He seemed to be everywhere, watching her every move.

Claire was at a loss. She didn't know how to stop this person, how to protect herself. She had tried the police, but they had told her that there was nothing they could do without concrete evidence.

In a moment of desperation, Claire turned to the private investigator who had helped her before. She explained the situation to him and asked if he could help her once again.

The private investigator agreed, but warned her that this time it would be much more difficult. He told her that the stalker was extremely clever and had left no trace of his identity.

Together, Claire and the private investigator embarked on a dangerous journey to unmask the stalker once and for all. They dug deep into his past, interviewed people who knew him, and followed every lead they could find.

As they got closer to the truth, they discovered that the stalker was not acting alone. He was part of a larger organization that was determined to take down successful women like Claire. They had been following her every move, waiting for the right moment to strike.

Claire and the private investigator knew that they had to act fast. They came up with a plan to expose the organization and bring them to justice.

In a heart-stopping conclusion, Claire and the private investigator executed their plan and unmasked the entire organization, including the stalker. Claire finally felt safe again, knowing that the people who had been tormenting her had been brought to justice.

But the experience had left her scarred. She knew that she could never truly be the person she was before the stalking started. She had to learn to live with the fear, the paranoia, and the trauma. But she also knew that she was stronger than she ever thought possible, and that she could face anything that came her way.

9 798889 758426

Printed by Libri Plureos GmbH in Hamburg, Germany